First published in 1944
This edition published by V&A Publishing, 2015

V&A Publishing
Victoria and Albert Museum
South Kensington
London SW7 2RL
www.vandapublishing.com

ISBN 978 1 85177 828 7

10 9 8 7 6 5 4 3 2 1
2019 2018 2017 2016 2015

Printed in China

V&A Publishing

Supporting the world's leading
museum of art and design,
the Victoria and Albert
Museum, London

BEN

written and
illustrated by
Jack · · · · ·
Townend

UNDER A SHED

in the corner of the Council yard at Upper Toddlington lived a steam-roller whose name was Ben. He was not a very happy steam-roller because never in all his life had he seen any of his brothers and sisters. He didn't even know if there were any other steam-rollers in the whole wide world and he often felt very sad as he sat there all by himself in the corner of the yard.

When Mr. Dodie was cleaning him up Ben felt much happier, but at night, when he was left alone, he always became sad again, and he often used to cry a little, leaving tiny pools of tears beneath his boiler. Then one day Mr. Dodie told Ben that the road from Upper Toddlington to Wibsey was to be made wider and that he would be needed to roll out the new road. Ben was so pleased at this, and next morning, when they set off, he felt very proud.

Through the town they went, Ben with his lamp high in the air, for he always held it like this when he was feeling happy. He had never been so far out of town before and he was thinking of all the new things which he might see. On they went until they reached the Wibsey road and here they stopped and set to work on the widening. Mr. Dodie put up a big sign saying, "DANGER, BEN AT WORK" just to warn anyone who might be coming along the road, and Ben laughed to himself as he rolled his way backwards and forwards over the stones.

At night time Ben was put at the road-side along with the tar-pan, the workmen's hut and the tool cart. He didn't like it very much because the workmen's hut, which had a wobbly wheel, creaked all the time and the tar-pan smelt so badly. But Ben soon fell asleep and dreamed, as usual, of other steam-rollers.

After a few days' work they reached the hilly part of the road, and one morning Ben saw in the distance a puff of white smoke. He held his breath and looked again. Could it be another steam-roller? YES IT WAS.

Ben gave a great roar and, leaving Mr. Dodie behind, he set off down the hill as fast as he could go. The other steam-roller, which belonged to the Wibsey Council, must have heard Ben's roar, for it raced down the other hill towards him.

At the bottom they met and Ben was so thrilled that he gurgled and spluttered until his boiler almost burst. The Wibsey engine was very beautiful, her chimney had a shiny top, her canopy had frills, and her name was Matilda.

At first Ben was shy, but he soon plucked up his courage and whispered, "Let's run away." To his great delight, Matilda answered, "Yes, let's." So they both took a very deep breath and with a loud whoop they left the road and raced across the fields as fast as their wheels would spin them. Down through the valleys they went, and over the hills until they came to a forest. They played here for a while and when night came they slept beneath the trees, and an owl came and sat on Matilda's chimney and two mice ate their supper on one of Ben's big wheels.

All through the night Ben and Matilda slept happily, but in the morning they were awakened by a great shout. Mr. Dodie and Mr. Longleg, Matilda's keeper, had come to take them back. Matilda began to cry, but Ben was very brave and very firm. He put on his brakes as hard as ever he could and declared that unless he could live with Matilda he would never, never work again. Neither Mr. Dodie nor Mr. Longleg liked the idea at all, but in the end they had to give in, for they couldn't do without Ben. So back to the road they all went and the next day two huts were built side by side,

one for Ben and one for Matilda, and a hole was made in the roof of each hut so that the two steam-rollers could put out their chimneys and breathe the fresh air. So Ben and Matilda are now very happy, for every day, when their work is done, they return to their little huts, where the owls hoot and the mice play, just as they did in the wood, and talk to each other till bed-time.

THE END